15.95

Miz Berlin Walks

Jane Yolen

ILLUSTRATED BY

Floyd Cooper

PHILOMEL BOOKS • NEW YORK

Patricia Lee Gauch, Editor

Special thanks to the Newport News Public Library System.

Library of Congress Cataloging-in Publication Data   Yolen, Jane.
Miz Berlin walks/by Jane Yolen; illustrated by Floyd Cooper.   p.   c.m.
Summary: Mary Louise gradually gets to know and love her elderly neighbor lady who
tells wonderful stories as she walks around the block of her Virginia home.
[1. Old age—Fiction. 2. Walking—Fiction.   3. Virginia—Fiction.]   I. Cooper, Floyd, ill.
II. Title. PZ7.Y78Mk 1997 [E]—dc20 95-45866 CIP AC
ISBN 0-399-22938-8   10 9 8 7 6 5 4 3 2 1   FIRST IMPRESSION

To the memory of my grandmother Fannie Berlin,
who just plain loved to walk —J. Y.

To Miz Taylor, my second grade art teacher,
who loved to walk —F. C.

Well, child, I recall once upon a time
an old woman lived on our street,
oldest woman I'd ever seen.
Her hair was white and fine
like the fluff off a dandelion.
Her skin was the color
of milk agate, like some marbles.
But old as she was,
Miz Berlin sure could walk.
Every evening, just before dark,
she would pass by our house,
going 'round the long block
that takes more than an hour
even if you go real fast.
And Miz Berlin, she went real slow.

On nice days she wore
a flowery cotton dress.
On cold days she wore
a blue button coat.
On rainy days she carried
a shiny black umbrella
with long silver ribs.
On hot days she carried a paper fan.
Oftimes she talked to herself
or sang little songs,
I couldn't tell which,
afraid to get too close, you see.
Old lady like that,
talking and singing to herself—
Mama always said:
"A body can't be too careful."

When Miz Berlin passed by
I'd watch her go all down the road
in that unhurried way,
talking or singing or
in quiet contemplation.
And then one hot summer eve,
because I had nothing else to do—
my best friend Frances Bird
having gone visiting kin in Roanoke—
I jumped off the porch swing
and ran right after Miz Berlin.
I expected her to yell "Scat!"
or to put a curse on me
or to fix me with her eye.
But all she did was walk on,
nodding and talking to herself.
She never once looked behind.

'Cept when I got close up,
she cleared her throat.
And then just as if we'd been conversing
she said: "Well, child, I recall the time
it rained feathers in Newport News.
I was a girl then, short and sassy,
just like some I could mention.
I was wading in the creek
hunting crawdaddies with Bubba,
when all about us
feathers began to fall.
Some settled on the creek bank
and some floated in the water,
like boats setting off
to Norfolk or Baltimore."
I felt like I was right there,
on the bank, in the creek!
Then we reached the corner,
and she stopped to take a breath.
I sighed and turned to go home.
I wasn't yet allowed
out of sight of our house.
But off Miz Berlin went,
still nodding and talking up a storm.

Of course, next evening,
right after supper,
I waited the longest time,
eating an ice cream on the porch.
I was fixing to ask her
what happened to those feathers
'cause I just *had* to know
the way the story ended.
The wind started up
brushing the treetops
with a faint *wist-wist,*
and suddenly there she was
coming up the sidewalk,
a paper fan in her hand.
I slipped off the porch
and followed her, step for step.
She seemed not to know I was there,
and started that story
right where she had left off.

"There was feathers to the right
and feathers to the left,
tickling my nose,
and falling on Bubba's head."
I finished my ice cream
and wiped my sticky hands
on my flower sunsuit.
Without missing a step,
without missing a word,
she reached back
and grabbed hold of my hand,
threading her fingers through mine.
We walked side by side then,
her telling more of the tale.
"So there I was in the creek, child.
Some of those feathers,
they were dove gray.
And some were crow black.
And some were dirty white,
like seagulls after the swill.
But one rained right into my hand,
and it was all over gold."

Just then we'd got to the block's end
and I had to go home,
no time for questions,
no time for the end of the tale.
Rules are rules, Mama says.
Next evening,
without even an ice cream,
I waited on the porch.
Didn't dare bounce my ball—
"A my name is . . ."—
or skip rope
for fear of missing her.
And suddenly there she was,
coming up the walk,
holding her silver-ribbed umbrella
high against the dark clouds.
I ran up and touched her hands
and we knitted our fingers.
"Was it an angel feather?" I asked,
scarcely able to breathe.
"Like as not," she said,
"for angels are partial to Newport News."

We didn't say a word more,
just walked along to the block's end,
both of us under the black umbrella
in the pattering rain.
Some stories take you that way.
Most evenings after that
I'd walk with Miz Berlin,
side by side,
step by step,
waiting cotton-quiet
till she cleared her throat.

Then if she said: "Why Mary Louise,
I smell the salt from the bay . . ."
I'd slip my hand into hers
and we'd talk of sailing ships—
cruisers on the Chesapeake
or pirate ships on the Spanish Main.
Or if she said: "Why Mary Louise,
I feel a soft summer breeze . . ."
we might speak of the hurricane of '48,
when water lapped like wet tongues
at the front steps of houses
all the way to Kecoughtan Road
and trees were bent near double.

But if she said: "Well, child,
I remember once upon a time . . ."
she'd tell a real whopper of a tale,
about clever Jack,
or that bad girl with a mouth full of toads,
or the ghost that walked each night
under the whispering trees.

Of course each story had to end
at the corner of the block.
I would run on home
stuffed full of tales,
which I told over and over
to my dolly
before falling asleep
in order to keep ahold of them.

Then one evening
in early March
—it was a false spring
when the blossoms on the trees
were furled tight as a baby's fist—
Miz Berlin told me the story
of her coming into the world.
It was a hard tale
full of hardscrabble dirt,
a two-room cabin,
and a lot of hunger.

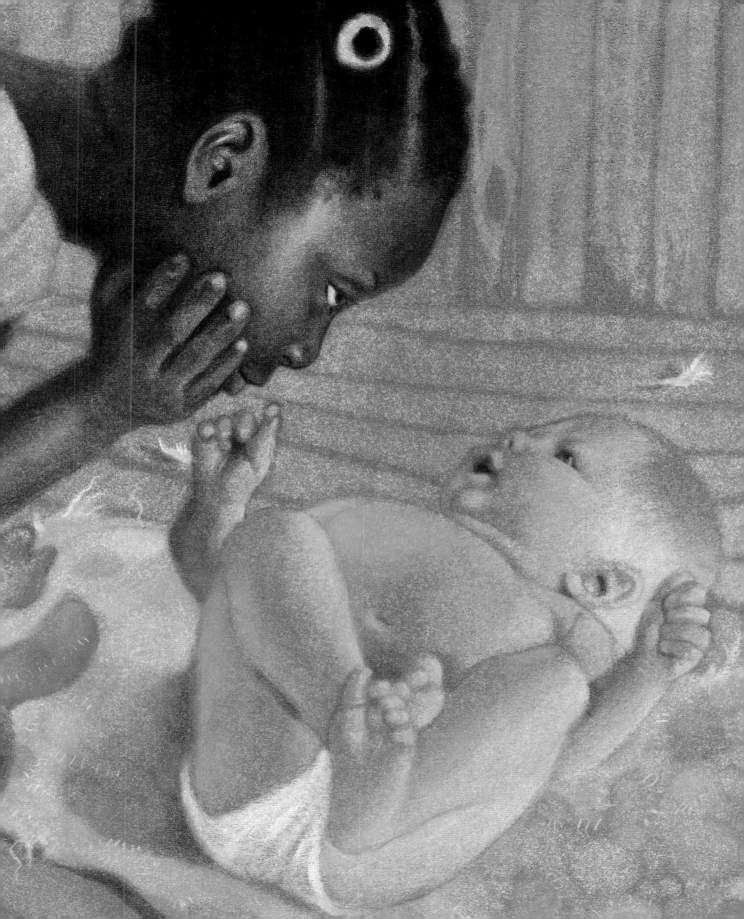

I waited all that next evening
for her to finish the story,
only she never came.
When I went way down the block
to where her house sat,
and up the walk first time ever,
the house was all dark
and the blinds drawn down.
I went back home
and cried in my sleep,
not knowing why.
In the morning my pillow
was spotted and damp.
Mama told me at breakfast
old Miz Berlin had fallen down the stairs.
Snapped her hip in two.
She was six weeks in the hospital.
When she came back to her own house
she still couldn't walk
and she couldn't talk, either.
I had to finish that story to my dolly
the best way I could.

Every evening after that
old Miz Berlin tried to rise out of bed
and then cried because she couldn't manage.
Leastways that's what her nurse said
when Mama and I brought over
one of Mama's famous straw-apple pies.
Miz Berlin up and died soon after,
and I think I know why:
even good habits are hard to break.
Hearts break so much easier.

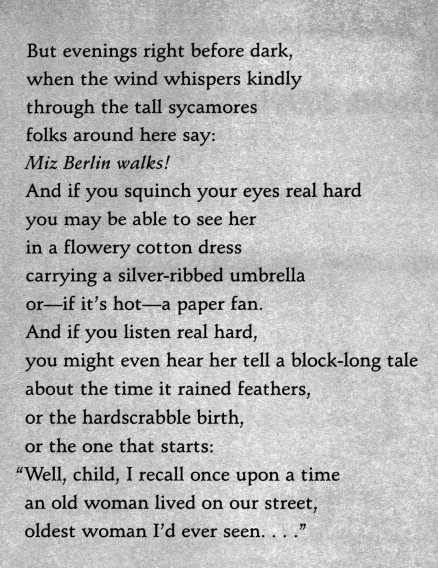

But evenings right before dark,
when the wind whispers kindly
through the tall sycamores
folks around here say:
Miz Berlin walks!
And if you squinch your eyes real hard
you may be able to see her
in a flowery cotton dress
carrying a silver-ribbed umbrella
or—if it's hot—a paper fan.
And if you listen real hard,
you might even hear her tell a block-long tale
about the time it rained feathers,
or the hardscrabble birth,
or the one that starts:
"Well, child, I recall once upon a time
an old woman lived on our street,
oldest woman I'd ever seen. . . ."